JUST PLAIN BOB

BUYING MY WIFE

Adult Erotica

WARNING

This book contains sexually explicit scenes and adult language. It may be considered offensive to some readers. This book is for sale to adults ONLY.

Please store your files wisely where they cannot be accessed by underage readers.

* * * * * * * * * * * * * * * * * * *

WANT FREE COPIES OF MY BOOKS?
Just visit my blog and download free copies of my books:
awesomeauthors.org/justplainbob

About the Publisher

4Fun Publishing, a member of **BLVNP Incorporated**, 340 S. Lemon #6200, Walnut CA 91789, info@blvnp.com / legal@blvnp.com
NOTE: Due to the highly emotional reaction of some people to works of erotic fiction, any email sent to the above address that contains foul language or religious references is automatically deleted by our anti-spam software and will not be seen. All other communications are welcome.

DISCLAIMER

Please don't be stupid and kill yourself. This book is a work of FICTION. Do not try any new sexual practice that you find in this book. It is fiction and not to be confused with reality. Neither the author nor the publisher or its associates assume any responsibility for any loss, injury, death or legal consequences resulting from acting on the contents in this book. Every character in this book is over 18 years of age. The author's opinions are not to be construed as the opinions of the publisher. The material in this book is for entertainment purposes ONLY. Enjoy.

Buying My Wife
Adult Erotica

By: Just Plain Bob

© Just Plain Bob 2015
ISBN: 978-1-68030-494-7

As the waiter led me to the table I wondered again about the phone call I'd received that Morning.

"Mr. Dalton?"

"Yes," I replied.

"My name is Jason Hargrove. I work with your wife and I was wondering if you could spare some time to discuss something that concerns her."

"What is this about, Mr. Hargrove?"

"I am at work right now and I can't really talk about it on the phone. Would it be possible for you to meet me for lunch today? Say around noon?"

I checked my planner and saw that I was free and being more than just a little curious, I told him that I could.

"Antoine's at twelve then?"

I told him I would be there and he told me to tell the hostess that I was meeting him. I spent the rest of the morning wondering why someone who worked with Abby would want to talk with me about something concerning her.

***

Abby and I had been introduced by a mutual friend at a surprise birthday party. Abby was a very good looking redhead, had a great sense of humor and seemed to like me and so before that party was over I had asked her for a date and she had said yes. The date went extremely well from my point of view so I asked her out again and again she said yes. After a half dozen dates we fell into a relationship that could almost be called "going steady."

I say "almost" because even though she spent most of her time with me she did go out on an occasional date with another guy. It irritated me when I would ask her what she would like to do on say a Saturday and she would say that she was having dinner with Tom, Dick, Harry or whomever, but I had not taken any steps to make us exclusive so I had no call on her time.

After two months of dating we had fallen into bed together and, happy to say, we were extremely compatible sexually and that fact only fed my irritation when she dated other guys because of my imagining her doing the same things with them that she did with me. I don't know that she ever did them, but I sure as hell didn't like thinking that she did.

The reason that I had not attempted to do something to make us exclusive was that I was afraid of marriage. I'd seen too many of my friends get married only to see them divorced a few years later. I could count on the thumbs of both hands the number of friends of mine who had marriages that had lasted longer than three years and none of the ones that had ended in divorce had ended amicably. Both parties had emerged bitter and resentful and I saw these things and it made me very hesitant.

On the other hand it was bothering the hell out of me that Abby was seeing other guys when I wanted her to be with me. One day I woke up to the fact that I was at my happiest when I was with Abby and I realized that if she kept seeing other guys, the day might come when she might decide that she liked one of them more than she did me.

I bought a ring, proposed and was devastated when she said no.

"I like you a lot, Rob. I like you an awful lot. Enough so that I spend the majority of my time with you, but I'm not ready to settle down yet."

It was a hell of a blow to me and I went home and sulked. I spent two days feeling sorry for myself and then I snapped out of it. "Fuck this shit!" I said to myself. "She isn't ready to settle down. She wants to date others? What's good for the goose is good for the gander." I had not dated (or even been interested in) another girl in the eight months I'd been seeing Abby. It was time to change that.

There were several single girls that worked in the same office I did and a couple of them had flirted with me from time to time. One day about a week after Abby had turned me down I walked into the restaurant where I usually have lunch and saw Jenny, one of the girls who had flirted with me, sitting in a booth by herself. I asked her if I could join her and she said yes. Before lunch was over I had a date with Jenny for that night when we got off work. It was just dinner and a few drinks, but I enjoyed myself so I asked her if she would go out with me again on Friday and she said yes.

Friday was dinner, drinks and dancing and I didn't get home until almost four-thirty in the morning. As I climbed into bed I thought about what had happened when I took Jenny home. Since it was only our second date and we were still in the "getting to know each other" stage I didn't try to kiss her goodnight when I walked her to her door. I told her that I'd had a great time and that I hoped we could do it again. As I turned to walk back to the car she said, "Hey!" I turned back to her and she threw her arms around me and gave me a kiss that made me weak in the knees.

"Does this mean maybe we can go out again?"

"You have my number and you know where to find me during the day."

I had just finished breakfast and was on my third cup of coffee when the phone rang. It was Abby.

"Where were you last night? I expected you to call and when you didn't I called you half a dozen times, but you never answered."

"Did we have something planned for last night?"

"No, but we usually do something."

"Well I guess that's partly right. We usually do something if you don't go out with someone else. But that is neither here nor there. The fact is you declined my invitation to make us exclusive and since you aren't ready to settle down and want to date other men, I decided after eight months of seeing no one but you, it was maybe time for me to date some other women. That's where I was last night. I had dinner and went dancing with a delightful young lady. I didn't get home until after four."

"Oh. Are we still on for tonight? You do remember that we are supposed to go to Britney's birthday party, right?"

From the tone of her voice I could tell she was upset with me. It was all right for her to see other men, but I was supposed to stay home? I was supposed to keep myself available for her? I had not realized that I was being taken so much for granted. Well, that was going to change.

"I haven't forgotten Britney's party. I'll pick you up at seven."

As I hung up I wondered just how things were going to go with me and Abby with me dating others.

I picked up Abby to take her to Brit's party and she was pretty quiet for the first part of the ride. About half way to Brit's she asked:

"Where did you go?"

"What do you mean?"

"Last night – where did you go?"

"Mario's for dinner and then drinks and dancing at The Pit."

"The Pit closes at two."

"Yeah, I know."

There were several seconds of silence and then Abby said, "You said that you didn't get home until after four."

Suddenly it dawned on me. The Pit closed at two, I didn't get home until after four so what did I do for those two hours? An evil streak that I never knew I had reared its head.

"Yep. About four-twenty, I think it was."

Was I going to tell Abby that Jenny and I stopped at Denny's for a bite to eat after leaving the pit? No way. Let her think that maybe something happened. After all, isn't that what she made me think when she went out with other guys? The rest of the ride was made in silence. When we got to Britney's the party was in full swing and Abby and I mingled. After a bit we separated as she saw a couple of girls she wanted to talk with and I ended up with a couple of guys talking football.

After a bit I moved on and I was talking with Pauline French when I noticed Abby watching us. She was talking with Carol and Bev, but her eyes never left me and Pauline. That evil streak of mine made another appearance and over the next two hours I made it a point to talk with every woman there who was single. Out of the corner of my eye I kept tabs on Abby and she never took her eyes off me.

Normally Abby and I are among the very last to leave a party, but we had only been at Brit's for three, maybe three and a half hours, when Abby came up to me and told me she was ready to leave. We walked around and said our goodbyes and then left. We weren't two blocks away from Brit's when Abby slid over next to me and her hand went to my zipper. That was something new. We had been making love for quite some time, but always at her place or mine. We had never done anything like what she was doing then. She unzipped me, worked my stiffening cock out of my pants and started stroking me.

"I am horny as hell, baby," she said, "and I want you ready when we get to my place."

I wasn't sure, but I thought that it was just possible that my going out the night before with someone else might have made Abby feel a little insecure in our relationship and she was trying to pull me back into the fold, so to speak. Not that I minded of course. What man was going to say no to a hand job from a beautiful and sexy woman?

Abby slowly stroked me for a minute or so and then she started to lower her head toward my lap. At that point I stopped her and told her to wait until we got to her place. She pouted, but I pointed out to her that giving me head while I was driving could cause me to lose my concentration and I might end up hitting someone or run off the road.

When we got to her apartment, she fairly pulled me along to her place and then to her bedroom. The love making was more intense than it had ever been before. It was almost as if Abby was trying to show me that no one could "do me better" and that I didn't need to see other women. And it just might have worked if my evil streak would have disappeared and stayed gone. But it didn't. In the morning Abby asked me if we could go to an art gallery opening on Wednesday and I thought for a second and then said that I couldn't do it. I was going to a cocktail party with one of the girls I worked with on Wednesday. It was total bullshit of course, but I wanted to hit Abby with some of the shit she had been hitting me with.

"At this moment I don't have any plans for next weekend if you would like to do something."

That she wasn't very happy with the situation I could tell, but she sucked it up and told me that she thought she could fill the weekend for me.

For the next three months Abby never put me off when I asked her what we were going to be doing on a given day and then one Thursday I asked her where she would like to go dancing on Saturday.

"Oh I'm sorry, honey, but I can't make it Saturday night. I've got something else going."

The next day at work I asked Jenny if she would like to have dinner with me that night and she said yes. We went to dinner and a movie and I asked her out again for Saturday and she said yes and I got a fairly hot goodnight kiss. When I got home I found a message on my answering machine from Abby wanting to know where I was and why I hadn't called her. I deleted the call and went to bed.

The phone woke me up at nine the next morning and caller ID showed that it was Abby calling so I didn't take the call and let it go to the machine.

"Rob, honey? It's Abby. Are you okay? I couldn't reach you yesterday and you didn't call. When you get this, call me, okay?"

I was just a little pissed at Abby right then so I unplugged the phone and turned off the answering machine.

That evening I took Jenny to the San Augustine Grill for dinner and then we went to the Boom Boom Room for drinks and dancing. We had been there for about an hour when Jenny asked me:

"Do you know that woman sitting in the booth right next to the hallway to the rest rooms?"

I looked over that way and saw Abby sitting there with some guy I'd never seen before. I turned back to Jenny and said,

"She's an old girlfriend. Why?"

"She hasn't taken her eyes off of you since she came in. Just how old of a girlfriend is she?"

"Depending on how you look at it either just before my first date with you or two days ago," and then I explained the situation to her.

"So I'm what, the stalking horse to get back at her."

"Of course not. I didn't know she would be here. I'm with you because you are the first girl I've asked out in over eight months and you said yes."

"So what do we do now?"

"We came here to have a good time and enjoy ourselves. If you don't think we can do that here now that Abby is here, we can go someplace else."

"No, I don't think so. If you are really through with her, letting her see you having a good time with another woman is one way of letting her know that you really mean it. Don't be surprised though if I push the envelope a little and make her think that we are a lot more intimate than we are."

"Why would you do that?"

"I used to date her male counterpart. We were a steady couple until he wanted to take out some bimbo. I finally had enough and I dumped him. All of a sudden I was the love of his life and he was ready to settle down if I would give him one more chance."

"What happened?"

"I took him back and married him. Two years later I caught him cheating on me and I kicked his ass out and divorced him."

"I never knew that you had been married."

"It wasn't the best time of my life and I don't usually talk about it. Anyway, from the way she is looking at you she is not all that happy to see you here with me so if you don't mind I'm going to work on winding her watch."

I smiled at her and told her to "wind away."

Jenny pulled me out onto the dance floor and for the rest of the evening while we were on the dance floor she was plastered against me with her arms around my neck. She pulled my head down and kissed me at least a dozen times. When we were sitting down she sat as close to me as she could and ran her hand up and down my leg. Out of the corner of my eye I watched Abby and it seemed to me that she wasn't having all that much fun with her date. Twice I saw him take her hand to pull her out on the dance floor and both times she jerked her hand away from him. And every time I glanced her way she was looking at Jenny and me. What Jenny was doing had a predictable effect on me and I spent a good part of the evening with an erection – an erection that Jenny was constantly rubbing against.

Finally it was time to leave and Jenny and I walked arm in arm past Abby's booth on the way out and my eyes met Abby's as we went by her. The look on her face said, "How could you do this to me?" Jenny said something and I turned to her and smiled and then Jenny and I were out the door.

Jenny was silent as I drove her home. I walked her to her door and she stood on her toes put her arms around my neck and kissed me. Then she released me and said:

"I'm sorry, Rob, I wasn't thinking ahead. What I did tonight made us both horny, but I'm not a slut. We haven't dated enough or gotten to know each other well enough for me to consider taking that step. I'm sorry that I got you all stirred up for nothing."

"Don't worry about it, Jenny. It was worth it to see the discomfort it caused Abby."

Jenny kissed me again and I headed on home. I stopped at Bud's Bar and Grill and munched popcorn and went through a couple of beers while I thought of my situation with Abby. I loved her – there was no doubt in my mind about that – but I couldn't take what was going on between us. She had said she liked me well enough to spend most of her time with me, but didn't want to settle down. I guess the bottom line was that I wasn't willing to settle for "most" of her time.

Well, I'd loved other things in my life that I had either never attained or had to give up and it looked like Abby was going to be added to the list. As much as I wanted her I was not going to play the game anymore. She wanted to date others, then let her. It was time for me to bite the bullet and move on. I closed Bud's and then stopped at the Village Inn for a bite and then headed for home.

As I turned into the driveway my headlights swept the front yard and the porch and I saw someone sitting on the porch steps. It was Abby. I got out of the car and walked up to the porch and I could see that Abby had been crying. She looked up at me when I started up the steps and said:

"Did you fuck her?"

The accusatory tone of voice pissed me off so I walked by her as I climbed the steps without saying a word. I was putting the key in the door like when she said:

"Well, did you?"

Without turning to look at her I said, "That is none of your business, Abby. I've never asked you how many of the guys you have dated have fucked you."

I went into the house and closed the door and then headed up the steps toward my bedroom. I was halfway up the stairs when I heard Abby trying to open the door. I'd turned the deadbolt to lock the door when I closed it and when she found the door locked she started beating on it and yelling:

"Damn it, Rob, let me in."

I went back down and opened the door. "What do you want, Abby?"

"I want you, Rob."

We were married three months later.

***

Fast forward eleven years and there I was approaching a table at Antoine's to talk about my wife with a man I didn't know. He stood as I approached and offered his hand and I took it.

"Thank you for coming. May I call you Rob?"

"Please do."

"And my name is Jason, but most people call me Jase. Shall we order?"

We both ordered the luncheon special with iced tea and when the waiter had gone I asked him just what the meeting was about. He took a deep breath and then said:

"This is awkward for me, but it is something that I just felt I have to do. I am in love with Abby and she has agreed to marry me as soon as your divorce is final."

I sat there looking at him too stunned to say a word and he took my silence to mean he should continue.

"I had expected that we would be married by now. Most divorces don't take a year, but Abby tells me you are fighting the divorce and throwing up roadblock after roadblock. Frankly I don't understand it. Why would you fight to keep someone who doesn't want you? Abby tells me that it is all about the money. She has agreed not to go after your pension or your 401k, but she remains firm on getting alimony and half of the other marital assets while you are just as firm on not paying her a cent of alimony and keeping the house instead of selling it and giving her half the proceeds. You also refuse to pay her attorney's fee. Do I have it right so far?"

Did he have it right? Hell no! What divorce? I had no clue as to what he was talking about. I didn't know what to say so I just stared at him and again he took my silence to mean that he should go on.

"We both know that what she wants is exactly what the courts will order since this is a no fault state and under no fault she is entitled to half of the assets. All you are doing is stalling to keep things from reaching a conclusion so you don't have to come up with the money to settle the case. I want this divorce settled so Abby and I can move on with our lives together so I've decided to see if I can't force the issue.

"I propose the following. I will pay Abby's attorney's fees. Alimony is a non issue in as much as it would stop when Abby remarries which will be the day after the divorce is final if I have my way. At most you would have to send her one check and if you have to do that I will reimburse you. That leaves the house. I had an independent appraisal done and while the appraiser couldn't gain access to your house he was able to compare it to similar house and come up with a market value. If it sold at the asking price after paying off the mortgage and all the fees and commissions, you would have forty-two thousand left which would then have to be split fifty/fifty with Abby.

"If you will cease fighting the divorce and allow it to go forward, I will write you a check for Abby's half of the proceeds which means that you will have the entire forty-two thousand for yourself."

I obviously had no clue as to what was going on. If Abby was suing me for a divorce I didn't know it. I hadn't been served with any papers and when I left the house that morning there hadn't seemed to be any lack of warmth in the kiss and "Have a great day" that I got from Abby. But Hargrove obviously thought he knew what he was talking about. It was time for me to go fishing.

"Everything you are proposing is okay with Abby?"

"Abby knows nothing about this meeting and what I am proposing. It is strictly between the two of us."

"How long have you and Abby been an item?"

"It would be about nine months now. Just after she caught you having your affair."

My affair? That was news to me. I hadn't had anything to do with another woman since I married Abby. I looked at him and said:

"I can't believe that she would have immediately taken up with another man."

"Oh no, I didn't mean to give you the wrong impression. It wasn't immediate. At first I was just a shoulder to cry on and things kind of developed from there."

I decided that I needed some time to find out just what the hell was going on so I said:

"I see. Well, as good as your proposal sounds, I'm afraid I can't accept it. I believe my house is worth a lot more than what your appraiser thinks."

"It doesn't matter to me. Whatever it turns out to be I will match Abby's half to insure that you get it all."

"You are serious about this?"

"Absolutely."

"Well Jason, I'm not a trusting guy. If you can put everything you just proposed into a legally enforceable document and sign it, you have a deal. It will say that you will pay Abby's attorney's fees, make me whole on the proceeds from the sale of the house and reimburse me for any alimony I have to pay until Abby remarries. As soon as I have that document in my hand and my attorney tells me that it is legally enforceable, I will withdraw all my objections to the divorce."

"I'll get on it as soon as I get back to work. Hopefully I will have it ready for your review by Friday. But one thing I insist on is that Abby never knows about this deal."

***

The first thing I did when I got back to my office was get out the Yellow Pages and turn to Investigators and Investigative Services. There were three within two blocks of my office and the first two I called couldn't see me for three or four days but the third one said, "Come on down." As I walked the two blocks to Acme Investigative Services I tried to think of what Hargrove must have been smoking. There was no way that Abby could be having an affair with him let alone be planning on marrying him. We were too happy together. We had a great relationship, but at the same time I couldn't help but feel that something made Hargrove approach me and the best way to find out what it was was to put someone on the case to check things out. Maybe Abby was just a good friend and he misunderstood her feelings. For my own peace of mind I needed to find out what was going on.

I met with Mr. Owen Paulson and filled him in on my meeting with Hargrove. I told him that I seriously doubted that my wife was being unfaithful, but I did need to know what Hargrove was up to. The only times Abby was out of the house were for her Tuesday night book club and discussion group, her Thursday night bridge club meeting and her Saturday morning beauty shop appointment to have her hair done while I played golf with three of my friends. I gave Paulson all the information he asked for regarding Abby and then I gave him a check to get him started. Since it was a Wednesday he told me they would put an operative on Abby Thursday morning when she left the house to go to work and then watch her until the following Tuesday. He told me I could stop by or call him Wednesday for a report.

As I walked back to my office I spent more time trying to figure out what Hargrove was really after. I had absolutely no doubt about Abby's love for me, but I could not figure out for the life of me what Hargrove's angle was.

Abby usually beat me home and when I got home that night she was in the kitchen fixing dinner. She stopped what she was doing, came to me and put her arms around me and kissed me. Dinner and dishes out of the way we curled up on the couch to watch some TV and Abby moved in next to me, put her head on my shoulder and cuddled up next to me. This woman cheating on me? No way!

***

Human nature being what it was, my talk with Hargrove had me taking a closer look at Abby, but I saw absolutely nothing that could make me even remotely think that she was having anything to do with Hargrove. She was as warm and loving as she had been on the day we took our vows. We touched, we kissed, we cuddled and snuggled and still, after eleven years, made love three or four times a week.

The following Wednesday at two in the afternoon Owen Paulson turned my life upside down. His operative had followed Abby when she left work Thursday night and went to an address on Perry Street. She didn't knock on the door or ring the bell, she just walked right in. It was ascertained that the house belonged to one Jason Hargrove. Abby entered the house, was inside for three and a half hours and then left and the operative followed her home.

Saturday I left the house at 6:45 to go play golf and ten minutes later Abby left and drove to the Perry Street address. She was inside for three hours and then she came out and drove to Wanda's House of Nails. An hour later she came out and drove home.

***

Tuesday she was followed from work to the Perry Street address where she remained for three hours until leaving for home.

"I need to point out that at no time was your wife actually seen with Mr. Hargrove. We do not even know that he was inside the house while she was there. For all we know she could be looking after her pets while he is away."

"How likely is that? The bottom line is that with the exception of Saturday when she does have a standing appointment at the beauty parlor, she was not where she was supposed to be. What can we do to find out for sure what she is doing?"

"There isn't much we can do. Entering the house to place audio and video devices would be illegal. About the best we can do is place some listening devices on your wife's person or in her car. We can also, with your permission, plant some surveillance equipment in your home."

"Do it. I have to know what is going on."

He gave me a bug to place in her purse – it was no bigger than a finger nail – and that night I told her to take my car to work because I was going to drop hers off at the shop on my way to work so they could do an oil change and a radiator flush. Paulson put a recorder in my car before I left his office and he put another in Abby's car after the oil change.

I took a half a day off work on Thursday and met Paulson and two of his people at the house and forty-five minutes later the house was wired. Then it was a case of sit back and wait.

It was not uncommon for Abby and I to make love when she got home after her "bridge club" meetings so it was not unexpected when I pulled Abby down on the bed that night. That night was different in that for the first time I was looking for something that would indicate that she had been with another man. Without calling attention to what I was doing I checked out her body for signs that she had been with someone else, but found none.

Oral sex was something that was a staple of our sex life, but when Abby went for my cock with her mouth I pushed her away and told her that I didn't feel like oral. That wasn't true of course, I always wanted head, but if I would have let her do me then I would be expected to do her and there was no way I was going to do that if she might have just come to me from another man's bed. It obviously wouldn't kill me because if she were cheating on me then I had already been doing it for a while, but I didn't know it then and knowing made all the difference in the world.

In my younger days before I met Abby I was a little wild and I had participated in a threesome or two and I'd been to a few gangbangs so I knew what sloppy seconds felt like and Abby didn't feel that way nor did she feel any looser or different, but then she never had. I started having bad thoughts about myself for doubting her. I began thinking that maybe there was a good explanation for her visits to Perry Street.

The next day at nine I received a call from Hargrove asking me if I was free for lunch. We met again at Antoine's and when we were seated he handed me a sheaf of papers. I looked through them and saw that it said exactly what I told him I needed it to say and that he had signed it and had his signature notarized.

"Looks fine to me. I'll have my lawyer look at it and if he finds no fault with it I will stop fighting Abby."

"May I ask you a personal question?"

"You can ask, but I won't promise you an answer."

"Abby is a marvelous woman. Why on Earth did you cheat on her?"

Since I had never cheated on Abby I had no real answer to the question so I just said:

"It was a drunken indiscretion. I didn't even know I'd done it until I woke up in the wrong bed the next morning."

"It may sound cruel of me to say it, but I'm glad it happened. Otherwise Abby and I wouldn't have ended up together."

When I got back to the office I tossed Hargrove's paperwork into my center desk drawer and forgot about it. It had only been something to buy me time and I was never going to use it.

***

Outside of wondering if Abby had paid a visit to Perry Street on Saturday morning, the weekend was the same as most others of the past eleven years. We made love Saturday night. Monday night we were sitting on the couch watching a new TV show ("Sam Who?") when Abby reached over and started rubbing my cock and it did what it always did when she paid attention to it. Abby said:

"Why don't we turn off the TV and see if we can't find something better to do."

Once again I thought, "No way this woman is cheating on me. She just couldn't be."

Tuesday I decided to stir the pot a bit. Over breakfast I said, "I've been thinking that maybe I should get some 'couth' in my life. I think I'm going to go with you to your book club meeting tonight."

Abby didn't bat an eye as she said, "You picked the wrong time to decide to pursue some intellectual enlightenment. The guest speaker had to cancel. But there is always next week."

That night in the middle of "Boston Legal" she cuddled up next to me and rubbed her tits into my arm. "Want to go play?" I did and so we did.

Wednesday at ten I got a call from Paulson telling me that he had something for me. As he passed the large manila envelope across his desk to me he said:

"This is the part of my job I hate. I'm always hoping that I can tell the client that his fears are groundless, but most of the time all I do is deliver bad news."

"It's bad?"

"I'm afraid so."

I made arrangements with him to let his people into the house to get their equipment, paid him the balance of what I owed and then I went back to work and called Abby and told her that I would be working late and not to hold dinner for me. When the office cleared out that night I took my briefcase and went to the conference room where there was a TV/VCR combo. I took the video and audio cassettes out of the envelope and set them both up to play. I already knew what I was going to hear because it had already been transcribed and I'd read the transcription.

The first section on the audio tape was from the bug in my car as Abby drove to work and talked on her cell phone. I only got one side of the conversation, but it was telling.

"Good morning, lover. I just wanted to hear your voice."

"I know, baby. Some day we will be able to do it openly at the office. Just be patient, baby, he can't stall much longer."

"I know, baby. I can't wait for Thursday either. I'm super horny too. I really missed being able to see you Tuesday night. I really hate it when I get those migraines. I'm almost to work. See you soon."

No room for denial after hearing that. The next section was from the bug in her purse.

(Sound of a door opening and closing).

"I'm here, lover."

"I'm in the bedroom."

(Sound of high heels walking across the floor).

"Oh my! Is that for me?"

"Indeed it is, my love. He has been hungry for you for days."

"Well I guess I'd better not keep him waiting any longer. Will you lick my pussy and get it wet and ready?"

"Silly girl! Don't I always?"

"You certainly don't need my mouth to get it hard, but I want to taste it anyway."

"Luckily we know how to do both at the same time. You want top or bottom?"

"I'll take the top. You sometimes get carried away when I'm on the bottom and I haven't yet figured out how to let that big thing get all the way down to my tummy."

(Sounds of oral sex).

"Enough, baby; I need you in my pussy."

(Sounds of love making).

"God, I really needed that. I love your big cock, baby."

"How about me?"

"You are a package deal, lover. The two of you come together."

"Is tonight the night? You keep promising me that you will stay the night one of these nights."

"I can't, baby. Rob is still checking up on me trying to catch me doing something he can use against me to stall the divorce. I know for a fact that he follows me to the library and the bridge club then goes to the apartment to see that I get home at the right time. I hope he never sticks around to see what time I actually leave the library and bridge club meetings. If he did and followed me here it could be another year before the divorce would go through. Oh look. He's ready for me again."

"Are you ever going to let me have anal?"

"I keep telling you, lover. I'm saving it for our wedding night. I can't give you my virginity, but I want you to have something special on our first night together as man and wife."

"I'm beginning to wonder if that is ever going to happen."

"Be patient, baby; it can't be too much longer. I've time for one more if you can get it up for me."

"With your help it shouldn't take long."

(Sounds of oral sex followed by sounds of love making).

"I've got just enough time to shower and douche. Want to scrub my back?"

"You still afraid that he will grab you and put his hand on your pussy to see if you are wet?"

"I don't put anything past him, lover. I'm just not taking any chances."

The next snippet was from the bug in her purse on Saturday morning.

"Morning, lover. Did you miss me?"

"Oh God yes."

(Sounds of kissing).

"Is that a roll of quarters in your pocket or are you just glad to see me?"

"Like you don't already know the answer to that. How much time do we have?"

"Three hours or so. I don't have to pick my mother up until eleven."

Next was a repeat of the sex that the two of them had on Thursday. Following their first fuck they discussed where they would honeymoon when they got married. Following their second fuck Hargrove asked how the divorce was moving along.

"He found a new one to use. He is now claiming that I have received commissions and bonuses that I secretly squirreled away and he has asked for additional time to discover them. Whether the court will grant his attorney that additional time I don't know."

"I've said it before, my love, and I'll say it again. Don't fight him. Give him whatever he wants. Walk away with nothing and just get it over with. I've got more money than we will ever need."

"I can't do that, Jason. He has turned it into a test of wills and I will not bow down to him. This talk is depressing. Cheer me up, lover. It feels like you are ready again. Make me scream!"

There was more, but I didn't care to listen to it. I put the video cassette into the TV/VCR combo and a picture came on the screen. The time stamp said that it was last Wednesday. Abby was in the kitchen fixing dinner. Her cell phone rang and she stopped peeling potatoes and got it out of her purse.

"Hello?"

"Fixing my mother dinner."

"I told you never to call me, Jason. What if my mother had picked up the phone?"

"I don't care."

"Because she is fond of Rob and thinks I'm making a big mistake in leaving him."

"No, Jason. The last thing I need is for her to start asking me who the men calling me are."

"No, Jason. I'll see you at work tomorrow."

She disconnected without saying goodbye and as she dropped the cell phone back into her purse she said:

"Jesus, what a stupid fucking twit!"

The tape kept running showing Abby working on dinner and five minutes later I came into the kitchen and Abby stopped doing what she was doing and greeted me with a big hug and a very hot kiss.

I leaned back in the chair and thought about what it all meant. There was no divorce in progress so Abby was obviously stringing Hargrove along, but why? What was with the 'lovey-dovey' shit when she was with him and the "stupid fucking twit" when she wasn't? She had

Hargrove so convinced that the two of them were going to ride off into the sunset together that he was willing to try and buy me off.

On my side of the coin I'd had a perfect wife for eleven years. She was loving and she spoiled me rotten. I could not point to anything that would even hint at trouble in our marriage. As an actress she was giving one of us – and quite possibly both of us – a superior performance. I couldn't speak for Hargrove, but I was not going to be handing out any Academy Awards, but I would be handing out something and that was for sure.

When I got home that night Abby greeted me with a warm hug and a kiss which I returned somewhat indifferently. Abby noticed and asked:

"Something wrong?"

"Just a bad day at work coupled with a headache. I think I'll swallow a handful of Tylenol and go to bed."

***

The next day at work I dug through my center desk drawer until I found the document that Hargrove had given me. I called Jim Barkly, an old school buddy who was a lawyer and asked him if he could meet me for lunch. He said he could and we met at Antoine's (only fitting since that is where Hargrove started it all). I explained the situation to him, gave him the document and asked him if it was legally enforceable. He read it and handed it back to me.

"As written it is doubtful you could win in court if this guy defaulted. The way it is written makes it sound like you are selling Abby to him. It would be a slam dunk if it were written along the lines of a promissory note. Change the wording to read, "In exchange for services rendered I, Jason Hargrove, promise that on the date that the dissolution of the marriage of blah, blah, blah becomes final I will pay to Robert

Dalton the following and then list what he is going to pay, but you have other options here."

"Like what?"

"This state allows legal actions for alienation of affections. With this document as proof that he is interfering in your personal life you could sue this Hargrove guy and win. You would probably get more out of it too."

"How so?"

"Assume he is right about the house. You would get forty-two thousand. Forget alimony. If you sue for divorce using infidelity as grounds Abby won't get alimony. On the other hand a suit for alienation of affections could get you up to two hundred thousand. The average award in a marriage of your length is around one hundred and fifty thousand. So, like I said, you have options. And of course there is a third option"

"And that would be?"

"You and Abby could stay together."

"After what she has done?"

"Come off it, Rob. You love her. You have had her on a pedestal since the day you married her and she loves you. It shows every time she gets within five feet of you. The woman can't keep her hands off you. I don't know what is going on with her and this Hargrove character, but it has not changed the way she feels about you. Once again, all I'm saying is that you have options."

Jim did not practice family law so I asked him for the name of a good divorce attorney and he gave me the names of three that he said were very good.

When I got back to my office I called Hargrove and told him that my attorney had shot down his document and I told him why. Hargrove told me that he would redo the document to address the attorney's concerns and then he said:

"I take it that once I redo the document and sign it we have a deal?"

"Not until the attorney looks at the revision and approves it."

"I'll have it to you by next Tuesday."

After I hung up on Hargrove I got out the Yellow Pages and looked up the names of the attorneys that Jim had given me and then I called the one closest to my office and made an appointment.

That night when Abby got home from her 'bridge club' I pulled her down onto the bed and fucked her twice. I was looking for some sign that she had been with Hargrove. I mean I knew that is where she had been, but I remembered her referring to Hargrove's cock as 'that big thing' and saying how much she "loved his big cock." I would have expected her to be a least a little loose coming to me straight from him, but she felt no different to me.

When we finished and Abby nodded off to sleep I stared up at the ceiling and made my plans. I did my best to keep myself under control through the rest of the week and weekend, but it wasn't easy.

***

Monday afternoon Hargrove called me and asked me to meet him for a drink after work. I met him at Barry's Irish Pub and he handed me the revised document. I looked it over and then said:

"It says exactly what my attorney said that it should say so I guess we have a deal. I expect that Abby will be bringing you up to date on the divorce by the end of the week."

I managed to get through Tuesday and Wednesday without losing it and I took Thursday off from work. By two that afternoon I had everything that I wanted out of the house. At three-thirty Abby was served at work and at three-ten my cell phone started going off as Abby tried to get in touch with me. I let all the calls go to voicemail and waited for the next act while I unloaded my stuff and carried it in to my new apartment.

At four-thirty Hargrove was served with the papers that informed him that he was being sued for alienation of affections in the matter of Dalton vs. Dalton.

At five I called Abby's cell phone and when she answered I said, "I got all your calls, Abby. What's up?"

"What the hell is going on, Rob? Why have I been served papers that say you are divorcing me? This is crazy, Rob. What are you doing?"

"You know that I love you, Abby. I love you more than life itself and you know that I will do anything and everything in my power to see you happy even if it hurts me. I've decided that to keep you happy I need to set you free so you can be with your true love. When you go to Jason's house tonight to spend your usual three hours with him you can tell him that you will soon be able to spend the rest of your life in his arms. It kills me to let you go, Abby, but your happiness is all that matters. Goodbye, my love."

I disconnected before I could start laughing. Even I realized that I was laying it on a bit thick. Almost immediately my cell went off and I turned it off and put it in my pocket.

The next morning when I got to work my secretary, who comes in a half an hour or so before I do, already had a dozen message slips for me. Seven of them were from Abby and one was from Hargrove. I tossed Abby's into the trash and told Janice what was going on.

"I don't like putting you in the middle here, Jan, but I am not taking calls from Abby. Tell her I've instructed you not to put her through or take her messages. Tell her I've taken a temporary assignment to Afghanistan and won't be back for six months or just hang up on her. It doesn't matter to me as long as I don't have to hear her voice."

I took Hargrove's slip into the office, sat down and gave him a call.

"What the fuck are you doing? What is the meaning of this suit? We had a deal!"

"We do. I did my part. I said I would move the divorce along and I have. Didn't Abby tell you about it when she made her weekly Thursday night visit to your house?"

"She didn't come last night, she didn't come to work this morning and she isn't answering my calls."

"All I can say is that you will need to get the story from Abby. My attorney told me not to discuss the matter to anyone and to refer all questions to him. Will you still be at work at ten this morning?"

"Yes. Why?"

"I'm sending you a copy of a video tape by special messenger. It will probably answer some of your questions. Good luck with Abby. Bye."

As I hung up the phone I felt at ease for the first time since my initial meeting with Hargrove. Troubled maybe, but still at ease since a load had been lifted off me. Troubled because Jim had nailed it. I was in love with Abby; I had had her up on a pedestal and I had no idea how I was going to live without her, but I couldn't live with her. I just wasn't the kind who could overlook what she had done. I might – just might – have been able to get by a one night's indiscretion, but an affair that had been going on three times a week for six months? No sir!

I left work early to forestall any chance that Abby might be waiting for me in the parking lot. I called Ben Davidson and told him I wouldn't be able to make it for our standing Saturday foursome. Abby knew the course we played so she just might have shown up. I'd have to talk with her eventually, but I wanted it on my terms and when I was ready.

The weekend was fairly uneventful except for my mother raising hell with me for walking out on "poor Abby" when I stopped by to have Sunday dinner with my parents and my sister.

"You have made that poor girl a wreck, Robert. I swear; I thought that I raised you better than that."

I shook my head in disbelief. "She cheated on me, mom! For six months now she has been seeing another man three times a week. What the hell am I supposed to do? Give her a medal?"

"You never gave the poor girl a chance to explain."

"I don't believe this shit," I said and I stomped out of the house. My sister followed me and on the front porch she said:

"Don't let mom get to you. She is naturally sympathetic towards Abby."

"Why in the hell would she be sympathetic toward a woman who has been cheating on her son for half a year?"

"Birds of a feather, I suppose."

"What does that mean?"

"You were too young at the time to know or understand, but mom cheated on dad. He caught her and somehow she managed to get him to forgive and forget. She likes Abby and she probably hopes that what worked for her will work for you and Abby."

"Fat chance of that happening."

"Why not? You know you love her. Everybody knows that she loves you."

"How the hell can she love me if she's running around stabbing me in the back?"

"I don't know. Ask her."

"You are as bad as mom."

"Hey! I'm not saying take her back. I'm just saying that you should talk to her. If for no other reason than I know you want to know why."

"Knowing why might only make it worse."

"Why would you say that?"

"You think my ego could take it if she told me it was because I couldn't satisfy her in the bedroom? I hear that and get to carry it around with me for the rest of my life? No thanks. I don't think so."

"It's your life, Rob, but I still think you need to talk with Abby."

***

The only message slip that Jan had for me on Monday morning was from Hargrove. As I took it I said:

"I don't see any from my about to be ex so I guess you must have found a way to shut her down."

"I just told her that you had instructed me not to take messages or put her through to you. And I hope you aren't upset with me, but I took it on myself to tell security that she isn't allowed any farther into the building than the reception desk."

"I think I'm going to have to give you a raise."

"Why thank you, Rob. It is nice to be appreciated."

Once at my desk I called Hargrove.

"Why did you send me that tape?"

"Why not? You ruined my life so why shouldn't I take a shot at ruining yours?"

"How did I ruin your life?"

"If you hadn't asked me to lunch and made me that proposition and dropped it on me that Abby was cheating on me I'd be a lot happier right now. She would still be stabbing me in the back, but at least I wouldn't know it."

"There never was a divorce?"

"You saw the tape. It had the date and time on it. Did that kiss look like something two people going through a divorce would be doing? Abby played both of us. The only divorce is the one I filed for last week."

"But why are you suing me? I didn't take her away from you. She lied to me too. I thought she was going through a divorce."

"Maybe, but she was still a married woman until the divorce was final and you knew it and you fucked her anyway."

"Why the charade with the legally enforceable document?"

"Evidence. Even though it is a civil action and not a criminal one I still needed evidence and the original and the revised documents clearly show that you were tampering with my marriage. I've got to get my revenge somehow and there you were. I got rid of her cheating ass, I make you pay and with any luck at all I've managed to poison the relationship between you and Abby so bad that working together will be hell for both of you and you will just have to suffer through it since she can't afford to quit now. Next time maybe you will wait until you have proof of the divorce before you bed the lady. Got a busy day ahead of me so I've got to go. Bye now."

After that call I had a smile on my face for the rest of the day.

***

The rest of the week was pretty uneventful. I got at least two calls a day on my cell from Abby, but I didn't take any of them.

Friday my mom called me and invited me to come to dinner on Saturday. It was not an abnormal request. Abby and I usually had dinner at mom's two or three times a month so I said I would be there. Saturday at five I drove up to my parent's house and saw Abby's car in the driveway so I kept on going. When I got back to my apartment I called my mother and told her that she could take the place setting for me off the table because I wouldn't be coming and then I told her that a good way to keep me from coming to visit her anymore would be for her to keep meddling in my life and then I told her to put Abby on. There was a short silence and then Abby came on the line.

"Rob, honey? Where are you? We need to talk. You need to let me explain."

"How in the hell do you expect to be able to explain to me why you stabbed me in the back three times a week for six months? Can't be done, Abby. Stop trying," and I disconnected.

On Tuesday my attorney called and told me he had been contacted by an attorney retained by Abby and it appeared that Abby was going to fight.

"She can't prevent the divorce, but she can delay it for quite a while. She is contesting the division of assets and making claims that you are hiding some assets. Are you?"

"Of course not. I guess we need to get nasty. How much trouble would it be to change the filing from Irreconcilable Differences to Infidelity?"

"Not much. We withdraw the original petition, wait one week and then refile."

"Do it. And then figure out what grounds we can use to sue Abby's employer for allowing two of their employees, one of them in management, to engage in an illicit affair. I know that they have something in their policies and procedures manual about things like that."

"I doubt that we could get anything there."

"I know, but a word to Abby and Hargrove that we are going after their employer may make Abby back off. If we bring their affair to management's attention it could get them both terminated and Abby and Hargrove know it. We might not get anything out of it monetarily, but the suit would become a matter of public record and I doubt that the company would want the notoriety so just the threat could work for us. I guess I will have to break down and talk with Abby and let her know what we plan on doing."

I called Abby and when she answered I simply said, "Barney's Pub tomorrow at six," and I hung up. The next day I was parked just down the street from the pub and I sat in the car and waited until a quarter after just to make Abby stew for a bit. I walked in and saw Abby sitting in a booth in the back. As I walked up to her she gave me a timid smile and I quickly wiped it off her face when I handed her an envelope with Paulson's report and copies of the audio tapes inside and said:

"Read the report and listen to the tapes and if you still think you might have anything to say that I will pay any attention to I'll call you Friday and set a time."

I turned and walked away from her.

***

The rest of the week was bad for me as one of the secondary effects of leaving Abby came into play. I had taken myself from three, four and sometimes five love making nights a week to nothing and I had done it overnight. I was suffering withdrawal and to make it worse my attorney had advised me to stay as pure as the driven snow until my divorce was final. It would not be wise to give Abby and her attorney anything that they could conceivably use against me.

What made it doubly bad was that Janice had apparently spread the word that Abby and I had split and several of the women I worked with were suddenly showing an interest in me. Janice herself was openly flirting with me and it was very hard to have to ignore her. Janice was a very sexy looking lady and she had recently gone through a divorce of her own. The rumors flying through the office were that she had caught her hubby in bed with her mother. I didn't know because there wasn't any way on God's green Earth that I was going to ask her.

But I was brave enough to ask her one question. Thursday we were in my office going over a proposal that she needed to type for me when I said:

"This is a pretty personal question, Jan, and you don't need to answer or explain why you don't want to answer, but I'm curious. Before I caught Abby cheating we had a pretty good sex life. I was used to making love on the average of four nights a week. I caught her, walked away from her and just like that I went from plenty of sex to nothing. You must have gone through the same thing when you went through your divorce. The sudden lack of sex has made me irritable and jumpy and my question is, how long before I start feeling like my old self again?"

She looked at me for several seconds and then said, "It never did go away. It stayed with me until my divorce was final and I was free to hook up with another guy."

"How long was that?"

"My divorce wasn't contested so it only took six months."

Then it was my turn to sit there silent for several very long moments and then I leaned back in my chair and said:

"Shit!"

"What's the matter?"

"Yours took six months and it was uncontested. My attorney called me the other day and told me that Abby was contesting the divorce. If it takes six months uncontested God only knows how long a contested divorce will take."

"So go find yourself a girlfriend."

"I can't. My attorney warned me against doing anything that Abby and her attorney could use against me."

"I guess it sucks to be you right now."

"Yeah, I guess it does. Where were we?"

"Paragraph four where you are discussing the need for soil samples."

I stayed busy for the rest of the day and at five Jan stuck her head in the door and said:

"It is quitting time, boss, and the herd is stumbling toward the elevators. You done with me for today?"

"Yes. Good night, Jan."

"Night, boss."

I finished up some minor paperwork, backed up my files and shut down the computer. I was just closing my briefcase when my office door opened and Jan came in. I looked at her with a questioning look, but before I could say anything she said:

"You said you were done with me for today, but I haven't even started on you," and she began to unbutton her blouse. "I checked the floor and everyone is gone. The cleaning crew doesn't get here until eleven and your ex, her attorney or any private detective they might hire can't get past the guard in the lobby. And, it just so happens that I am between boyfriends." By then she was down to a thigh highs, heels and a thong. She spun around in front of me and asked, "What do you think?"

I answered her by standing up and pulling my zipper down. The first time I did her from behind as she bent forward over my desk and the second time it was with her lying on her back on my desk. The third and final time I was sitting on my chair as she rode me like a stripper giving a lap dance. As we were getting dressed she said:

"You leave first and I'll wait fifteen minutes before I leave. That way if anyone is outside watching for you, you will draw them off and they won't be there to see me leave."

"Thank you, Jan."

"Don't thank me, boss. I told you I was between boyfriends and I needed it just as bad as you did. You up for a friends with benefits relationship as long as we keep it here in the office in the evenings?"

I smiled at her and said that I found that to be a very nice idea and then I headed for home. As I drove I wondered if I should feel guilty about what I'd just done with Jan since I was still a married man, but then I thought that Abby had been doing it for the last six months and decided "No way." I wasn't even close to be even.

When I got to my apartment I called Abby on her cell and when she answered I just said:

"Barney's at six tomorrow," and hung up.

***

The next evening I didn't waste any time playing mind games. I walked into Barney's at six on the dot and saw Abby sitting in the same booth in the back. I walked over and slid onto the bench seat across from her.

"Okay, Abby. Go ahead and say your piece."

"Can't we go to some place a little quieter and private?"

"No. My attorney told me that I shouldn't talk to you at all without him being present, but I figure if we do it where there are plenty of witnesses you won't be able to pull anything."

"Pull anything? Like what?"

"Who knows? If we were alone you could accuse me of saying or doing something that might make you look good and me look bad and it would just be my word against yours. Here, out in the open and with plenty of people around I don't have to worry so much."

"Has it come to that? I love you, Rob, and I would never hurt you like that."

"You love me and you wouldn't hurt me? Just what the fuck do you think your stabbing me in the back with Hargrove did? Do you think it made me feel good? You think it didn't hurt to find out that the woman I loved was cheating on me and had been doing it three times a week for over six fucking months?"

"Of course I know it hurt you, Rob, but I never meant for it to hurt you. What I meant was that I would never deliberately hurt you. The thing with Jason wasn't supposed to hurt you. You were never supposed to know. I was very careful to keep from doing anything that would let you find out. It was just going to be a brief fling and you would never know about it. How did you find out?"

I told her about meeting Hargrove and about the proposition he made me.

"That asshole!"

"That's no way to talk about the man who was in such an all-fired hurry to marry you although I don't know how anxious he is to marry you now since I slapped him with the alienation of affections suit."

"We haven't talked since the day you served me with divorce papers."

"Good. I was hoping I could poison the relationship between the two of you. Back to why we are here. You said we needed to talk. I don't know why because I have nothing to say, but go ahead and speak your piece."

"You are making it sound like nothing I say is going to change anything."

"That about sums it up."

She looked at me for several moments and then said, "At least I have to try. You know I love you, Rob, at least you should. I've shown it every day for the last eleven years. Think about it, Rob. Have you not been happy for the last eleven years? Until Jason called you didn't you have a great life? The cuddling, the snuggling, the love making, the love and affection were all there. Wasn't I everything you wanted in a wife? Did I ever say no to you on anything? Did I not do my best to spoil you every day we were together? Give me honest answers to those questions, Rob. Was I not everything you could want?"

She had me there. Up until I met Hargrove for lunch my life had been perfect. But I HAD met Hargrove for lunch. It was a couple of seconds before I answered her.

"Yes, Abby, I liked my life before talking to Hargrove, but the operative words there are "before I talked to Hargrove." That talk changed things in a big way. There is just something about finding out that your wife is a cheating whore (she winced at that) that changes your outlook on life. In the space of fifteen seconds you go from fat, dumb and happy to insecure and the questions start. Why? What did I do wrong? Why wasn't I man enough for her? What does he have that I don't? How long has it been going on? Is he the first or just one of many? Has she been cheating all our marriage? Is the way she acts around me just that – an act? Is it her way to keep me from becoming suspicious? Has she ever played bridge on Thursdays? Has she ever gone to a book discussion group meeting in her life? Did I need to get checked for sexually transmitted diseases? The answer to that one was yes and I did it the day I moved out. So far I'm free, but I need to wait about six months before I'll know about the possibility of Aids.

"Then I had to wonder about things like how much of a kick did you get out of fucking me just after leaving him? When I fucked you, were you thinking of him? Was it me who gave you the orgasms or the memory of what you had just done with him? Did you ever make me taste him? Did you ever have me eat your pussy after fucking him just to see if you could get off on having me lick your well used pussy? I know from the tapes that you shower and douche before you come home, but when did you start doing that? After you had fed me his leftovers a couple of times and then decided you had better stop before you got caught?

"No, Abby, it does not matter a rat's ass what my life was like before I talked to Hargrove; what it is like now is what matters and right now it sucks."

"I swear to God, Rob, that Jason was the only one and I never came to you from him that I wasn't showered and douched. And I never, ever, not even once, thought of him while I was making love to you. The answers to your other questions are no, you did nothing wrong and you are more than man enough for me."

"It doesn't matter what you say now, Abby, because I have no reason to believe anything you say. You have been lying to me for the last six months so I have no reason to believe you now. Anything you say now will be self-serving as far as I'm concerned."

"Please, Rob, I do love you. Please let me explain why I did what I did. If you know that you will understand that it has nothing to do with my love for you."

"I'm here, Abby, and this is the only time you will get to speak your piece to me so go."

"It happened because I got curious and I let my curiosity get the better of me."

It was one of those strange moments. I really didn't want to know about what Abby did with Hargrove – she was a cheating bitch – but at the same time I was wanting to know why she had turned my life to shit. Curiosity won out and I said:

"Explain that."

"Girls gossip, Rob, they gossip a lot and if among friends they will gossip about anything and everything. Jason came to work for us about two years ago. After a couple of months he started dating some of the other girls in the office and it wasn't long before the girls were gossiping about how good he was in bed. It was rumored that he had a very large cock and that he knew how to use it. Then the gossip for the most part shifted to who Jason would go after next. He went with one for about six weeks and then he would move on to another one. A couple of the girls said they wouldn't mind making it permanent, but Jason said he was a long way from wanting to settle down. We all watched who he went with and speculated on how long she would last.

"I watched with the others and as I watched I began to ask myself what was wrong with me? I looked at myself in the mirror looking for blemishes or anything that might make me seem unattractive. In my mind I was the best looking woman in the company, but Jason never seemed to look at me twice. Not that I really wanted him to of course, but it was still my ego working on me. I was better looking than any of the girls he went out with so why wouldn't he even talk to me. It ate at me for a couple of months and then one day I said, "I'll make him notice me."

"Again, I didn't plan on having an affair or a one night stand or anything like that; it was all about me being pissed off about being ignored. I started flirting with him. If he was alone at a table in the break room I would join him. We talked about the job, fellow employees and management and got to know each other a little, but my goal was to get him to ask me out. I would say thanks, but no thanks, but my ego required that I at least get him to ask.

"Weeks went by with nothing happening and I was getting pissed off and frustrated over the fact that the best looking woman in the office couldn't get his attention. And before I start sounding too stupid I do realize that maybe I'm not the best looking woman working for the company, but I am in the top ten. Anyway, the day came when I forced the issue. I flat out asked him why he had never hit on me. His answer was short and to the point.

"Because you are married."

"By then I was on a mission and while his reason was one that you would expect from a nice guy and a gentleman I was past caring about that stuff. My goal for months had been to affirm my desirability by getting Jason to ask me out so I said:

"Maybe technically, but not actually."

"He asked me how that could be and I told him that we were separated and going through a divorce. We talked some more and I made up a story about catching you in bed with a friend of mine. Break was over by then and we had to get back to work. He asked me if I would like to meet him after work for a drink and I said yes. We got together several times over the next couple of weeks and I whined about how rotten you were and how unfair life was and all the time I was working on getting him to ask me out on a "real" date. Not a stop for coffee or stop after work for a drink date, but a real, "Will you have dinner with me and maybe go for a couple of drinks and some dancing" type date. As soon as he asked me I would say no, but I had to – just had to – get him to ask me for that date.

"I stated complaining about not having any social life at all. I kept saying how nice it would be if I could go out dancing some night just to have a little fun and then one day he took the hint and asked me for a date and I got stupid. Instead of just saying no thanks I convinced myself that I had worked hard to get him to ask me out and that I owed myself a reward for that hard work. I'd go on the date and then it would be over. I would have won! That is how I was seeing it then – a contest that I had won.

"We went out for dinner on a Tuesday night and then stopped for a drink. We danced to a couple of songs and then he dropped me off at my car. I kissed him on the cheek and then drove home smiling. I had done it! But then I got to thinking, did I really do it? Had he asked me out because I was a desirable woman or because he felt sorry for me after my telling him my tale of woe? That wasn't winning. He had to ask me out because he wanted me before I could say that I'd won.

"He asked me out a second time and the date was the same as the first. Dinner, some drinks and a kiss on his cheek when I thanked him for a nice time. I was pissed as I drove home. What was wrong with him? He wouldn't dance close, his hands never strayed and he didn't even try and kiss me goodnight. Why didn't he find me desirable? What did all those other women he dated have that I didn't? I said yes to a third date and that time I pushed things. When we danced I pressed in close. I rubbed my leg on his and I felt him start to harden. Yes! He did want me. I rubbed against him every dance and when he dropped me at my car he kissed me. It was a hot, passionate kiss. He wanted me; he desired me and I could finally put an end to things.

"Except on the way home I started thinking that I had it all wrong. All he did was respond to me. He got a hard on because I tried to give him a hard on. He still had not come after me. The next date was different. On the dance floor he let his hands wander. He cupped my ass. He brushed my breasts. And when he dropped me at my car he pulled me into his arms and kissed me. His tongue slipped into my mouth and I was ecstatic. HE WANTED ME! Everything he did that night he did because HE wanted to do it. The game was over and I'd gotten what I wanted. My ego was satisfied.

"Then I got stupid again.

"The girls wanted to know all about my dates with Jason. "Is he as good a lover as we hear? Is his penis really as big as rumor has it?" I really had no idea, but if I would have said that I would have lost face with the group. Everyone else he had dated had raved about him and if I would have told them that nothing happened they would all be looking at me and wondering why I wasn't woman enough for Jason. So I lied. I told them he was magnificent, a real stud and yes indeed he had a big cock. That should have been the end of it, but it wasn't.

"He asked me out again and I turned him down. Two days later he asked me again and again I said no. He asked me why and I couldn't tell him the real reason why I went out with him in the first place so I lied to him and told him that I thought I was falling for him. Then I told him that my life at the time was already in too big of a mess for me to become attached to another man. Then he told me that he was falling for me too and he thought that we should give things a try as he thought we had a great future in front of us. I told him sorry, but I wasn't even close to being ready to go there.

"He kept asking me and I kept saying no. I thought he would eventually get the hint and move on to another girl, but he kept after me. What made things worse was that we worked together and saw each other every day. Things began to get awkward at the office. Then I got the bright idea that I would go out with him again, come up with a reason to have a big nasty argument and then tell him to fuck off and leave me alone. He didn't do anything on that date that I could use, but I needed him to keep dating me until he did give me something so when he dropped me at my car we kissed for a bit. The next date he gave me nothing to use so when he dropped me at my car that night we sat in his car and necked for a while. The next date the necking got a little hotter and I kept waiting for him to run his hand up my leg or up under my blouse so I could slap him down, tell him I wasn't some cheap slut, that I never wanted to see him again and then get out of his car. But he never did anything but hug and kiss me.

"The next date I wore a short skirt and heels and I didn't wear a bra. My blouse was low cut and he could see plenty of cleavage. I thought for sure that the way I was dressed would fire him up and lead him to take some liberties, but again all he did was hug and kiss me. I had to lead him on until he gave me something I could use against him so I kissed him back and some of those necking sessions got pretty damned steamy. I finally reached a point where I felt I had to make something happen. It was another one of my stupid moves.

"My plan was to go after him. I'd work his cock out of his pants and start to give him a hand job. I'd lower my head real close so it would look like I wanted to get a good look at him cumming. I would make sure that his cock would feel my hot breath and then I depended on him to do what most men would. He would put his hand on the back of my head and try to push it down so I would suck his cock. When he did that I would explode in a rage and things would finally end. I'd give him a dirty look every time he got near me at work and eventually he would keep his distance and ignore me.

"It was a bad plan. I got his cock out and started to stroke it. When I lowered my head for the second part of the plan I was surprised. He was uncut! He had never been circumcised. I had never seen an uncut cock and I was fascinated. So fascinated that I didn't even notice when Jason pushed my head down. I unthinkingly opened my mouth, took him in and then it was too late. I sucked him off.

"I cried all the way home. I never considered the dates cheating on you, but there was no way I could look at that blow job the same way. I had cheated on you and it was killing me. Thankfully you were asleep when I got home since I didn't have a clue as to how I could explain my crying. I stayed awake the entire night staring up at the ceiling and cursing myself for getting myself into the mess I was in. The next day was Friday and I called in sick because I couldn't bear to look at Jason. I hated him for what he had done to me. I know, I know, he hadn't done anything to me – I did it all to myself – but I wasn't thinking too clearly at the time.

"I spent the weekend trying to figure out how I was going to get myself out of the hole I'd dug. Instead of coming up with a reason to use to slap Jason down all I had done was to give him even more reason to keep after me. I just had to come up with a way to turn Jason away from me. So naturally I did what I seemed to do best. I came up with another stupid idea. I had already cheated on you once and it hadn't killed me and you had no idea so I'd do it one more time. You would never know and I'd solve the Jason problem once and for all.

"I'd let him fuck me. I wouldn't say anything about a condom and he had no way of knowing that I was on the pill. I'd wait until he was going good and then I'd tell him I wasn't protected and make him promise to pull out when it was time to cum. He would promise and when the time came he would be so into trying to get off that he wouldn't think of it. He would cum in me and I would call him a fucking pig and then tell him that I never wanted to see him again.

"I waited for you to go on one of your out of town business trips and the second night you were gone I gave myself to Jason. Everything went just like I planned. He promised to pull out, didn't and came in me. Only one problem – when he came in me I had the biggest and strongest orgasm of my life and I wanted another one just like it so I sucked him hard and we did it again and I had another huge orgasm. And no, before you ask, it wasn't because of his big cock and it wasn't because he was a great lover. It was because what I was doing was so deliciously wicked and exciting – I was getting off on the cheating.

"Jason's cock by the way is only an inch and a half longer than yours, but you are almost twice as big around and I like yours so much better than his. And you are by far a better lover, but the orgasms I got when I was with Jason were out of this world. They were so stupendous that I kept wanting more and more of them. I fell into seeing Jason two and three times a week just so I could experience more of them.

"Jason is a nice guy, but as a person he doesn't mean anything to me. Since the orgasm was coming from the cheating I could have dropped Jason and gone to someone else, but I didn't want to do that. I really didn't to be with Jason, but I did want those mind blowing orgasms so I kept seeing him. Then he started in on the when can we get married stuff. No way was I going to leave you; not even to keep getting those orgasms, so I kept on lying to Jason about how slow our divorce was moving. Eventually I knew I was going to have to break it off with him even if it did mean that I would have to give up those orgasms, but I kept stalling and stalling and ignoring the way he kept getting more and more possessive. Instead of ending it when he started getting possessive I kept saying "just one more time, just one more orgasm.' And here we are."

"And now what? I'm supposed to say "Gee, that makes me feel a whole lot better knowing that she likes my cock more than his and that she says I'm a better lover than he is." Boy, am I ever relieved to know these things. I guess we can get back together and move on with our lives. Is that it?"

"I can hope."

"Give me one good reason why I should offer you any hope after what you have done."

"I love you and you know it. And I know you love me even though I did something absolutely and terribly stupid."

"I can't argue that with you, Abby. I do love you, but love sometimes isn't enough and this is one of those times. You took eleven years worth of trust and tossed it into the trash can. I can never trust you again. You said it yourself. You knew you should end it, but you kept stalling so you could have one more time – one more orgasm. Now that Jason is out of the picture how long will it be before you hook up with another guy so you can have just one more of those humongous orgasms? I know you will tell me that there is no way that you would ever do it again if I will just forgive you, but can I trust you enough to believe you? No I can't. For six months now you have been lying to me about where you were going and what you were doing. For all I know you are lying about me being a better lover and your liking my cock better than Jason's. I can't believe anything you tell me, Abby.

" I'll always be thinking that someday you will convince yourself that it wouldn't hurt any if you snuck away to have one – just one – of those marvelous orgasms. I could never enjoy myself at a party or dance because I would be watching you like a hawk to see that you didn't try to sneak out with someone for a cheating quickie. Every time you would come home late I'd be wondering if it was because of a quick backseat coupling. Would your "girls night out" be with only girls? I'm sorry, Abby, but I can't live like that. You can promise me that it will never happen again and really mean it when you say it, but if just the right circumstance happens and you think you could do it and no one would ever know? The trust is gone, Abby, and I would always be looking for the signs that you were cheating again."

"I'm sorry, Rob. I never meant for this to happen."

"I'm sorry too, Abby; more than you will ever know. Now, I've listened to what you have had to say and it is your turn to listen to me. My attorney says you are going to fight the divorce. You need to rethink that. You are going to need your job and if you fight the divorce my next lawsuit will be against your employer for not enforcing the provisions in the employee handbook concerning fraternization of employees. Jason is in management and company policy is quite clear on what you and Jason were doing. It is a clear no-no. How long do you think you will remain employed if I sue your company? If you fight the divorce, Abby, all you can do is slow it down. Eventually it will be granted so how much do you want to lose just to slow things down a little?"

I got up and left her sitting at the table crying.

***

Two days later my attorney called me and told me Abby had withdrawn her counter-suit. I don't know if she talked to Hargrove or whether he figured it out on his own, but three days later he offered to settle.

It took six months for the divorce to become final and for five of those months I enjoyed my FWB relationship with Jan, but then she met a guy who she thought had possibilities so we parted as friends. Abby called once every two weeks and asked if maybe I had reconsidered and I always told her sorry, but no.

Three weeks after the divorce was final, Abby called and I told her that I hadn't changed my mind and she asked me what I was doing for a sex life. I told her I didn't have one and she told me that she didn't have one either and then she hit me with it.

"I miss you, Rob. I want you back in my life. If it can't be as a husband, how about as a boyfriend, a lover, a kind of friends with benefits type thing?"

So that is where we are now. We see each other three or four times a week. Sometimes we spend the night at my place and sometimes at hers. I know that she is hoping that sometime in the future, if we keep doing what we are doing, we will get back together, but it isn't going to happen. Time isn't going to change the fact that I'll never trust her again and as I've already told her I will not live my life watching her every move to see if she slips off again.

I still love the stupid cunt and I will go with the FWB arrangement until the day I die if she is willing to keep things that way. It is just too bad that Abby never realized that once the trust is gone it is never going to come back.

The End

Here is a sample from another story you may enjoy:

JUST PLAIN BOB

Gail's
PRICE
ROMANCE EROTICA

I walked up to Gail and Norm and keeping my voice low, but still full of menace I said:

"Get your fucking hands off of my wife's ass before I rip your arm off and shove it up your ass!"

His eyes got big and her let go of Gail and stepped back as I said:

"I'm cutting in and you would be wise to make yourself scarce."

"How dare you embarrass me like that?" Gail hissed at me.

"Where the hell do you get off humiliating me in front of my friends and family by letting some asshole play with your ass in front of them?" I snarled right back at her.

Her eyes got big and the look on her face said as clear as day: *Whoa!! Where did that come from?* She had never had me speak to her before in that manner and in that tone of voice and it flat took her by surprise. She moved in close and buried her head into my chest like the new bride that she was and I wondered if we would have words on the way to the condo or after we got there. I didn't intend to carry it any farther if she dropped it, but she would get both barrels if she copped an attitude.

I had expected a glorious first night with my bride, but after what I'd heard and seen in the last hour, a ration of shit from Gail could damned well lead to an annulment attempt on Monday morning. Sooner if I could find an attorney open on Sunday.

She had eased my mind a bit when she whispered, "How much longer before we can get out of here? I want you, baby. I've waited long enough. You've kept your promise and it's time."

"We can leave whenever you want. All the duty dances are done with and everyone knows that our flight to Aruba leaves early so it won't surprise anyone if we leave."

"Now. I want to leave now."

We made the rounds and said our goodbyes and then headed for home.

Over the last couple of days we had gotten, Gail moved into the condo, so the condo was "home" for Gail now. She had of course been there many times, but I still performed the ritual "carry the new bride over the threshold" thing, and as I did it Gail said:

"Straight to the bedroom, baby. No stops along the way."

Gail and I had never seen each other totally naked. I'd seen her naked from the waist down when I had eaten her out and she had seen me with my pants and briefs down to my knees when she had sucked my dick. We had seen each other in swimming suits and Gail in a bikini was an instant wood generator. I'd known that what I was getting was 'choice,' but even so, seeing her totally nude for the first time was breathtaking.

"Sit down on the bed, baby," Gail said and so I did. She knelt in front of me and said, "I do not want our first time to be a quickie, baby. I want it to last so I'm going to get the quick one out of the way."

She lowered her head and took my meat in her mouth.

If you enjoyed this sample then look for **Gail's Price**.

Also by this Author:

The Prodigal Family: The Abbotts

Watching My Shared Wife

The Waitress and the Runaway Husband

Baiting Mr. Little

Too Hot for Henry

Chuck's Fantasy

The Redhead's Desires

Rescued at Riley's

His Every Fantasy

Open Mike Night

Pursuit for Revenge

Why Does He Do That?

Halloween & Drugs

Tracey

When Rob Met Kari

Becoming a Shared Wife, Vol. 1 –
(Wife Sharing and Other Adventures)

Becoming a Shared Wife, Vol. 2 –
(Hazardous Wives)

Becoming a Shared Wife, Vol. 3 –
(Wives Who Stray)

Becoming a Shared Husband, Vol. 1 –

(Suck Me)

Becoming a Shared Husband, Vol. 2 –

(Husbands Who Stray)

Becoming a Shared Husband, Vol. 3 –

(Get even!)

Becoming a Shared Couple, Vol. 1 –

(Steamy Swingers)

Becoming a Shared Couple, Vol. 2 –

(The Share Thing)

Becoming a Shared Couple, Vol. 3 –

(Kathy is Wild)

Erotica Short Stories, Vol. 1 –

(Taboo Desires)

Erotica Short Stories, Vol. 2 –

(Nasty Steps)

Erotica Short Stories, Vol. 3 –

(Married But...)

Erotica Short Stories, Vol. 4 –

(Sizzling 10)

Erotica Short Stories, Vol. 5 –

(In My Wife's Panties)

Erotica Short Stories, Vol. 6 –

(Taboo Unlimited Desires)

Erotica Short Stories, Vol. 7 –

(XXX Stories)

Her Illicit Adventures

What I Want To Do To Her

Too Fun To Give Up

Creamed

Stepping Out

Hottest Wife

Naughty Wives

Deepest and Darkest

More Than She Can Take

Jennifer's Toes

The More The Sexier

Spice Up

Cyndi

Naughty And Nice

House Of Lovers

Hungry For More

Sweet Revenge

Turning Mommies Wild: The Carriage Tales

Bought And Used

Get Me Off

The Gambler

Gail's Price

From the Author

WANT FREE COPIES OF MY BOOKS?

Just visit my blog and download free copies of my books:
awesomeauthors.org/justplainbob

Yes, I write about sluts and whores because as everyone knows, you tend to write about the things you know. And I do like sluts and whores, just not the ones that lie to me and cheat on me.

So be forewarned - if you click on a Just Plain Bob story you will be getting sluts, whores and husbands who do not kill, maim and destroy. There are other things you will rarely find in a Just Plain Bob story.

If you enjoyed any of my books then please share the love and promote my books in Amazon. I would really appreciate your honest reviews, too!

Good news is always welcome.

One Last Thing, For Kindle Readers...

When you turn the page, Kindle will give you the opportunity to rate this book and share your thoughts on Facebook and Twitter. If you enjoyed my writings, would you please take a few seconds to let your friends know about it? Because... when they enjoy they will be grateful to you and so will I.

Thank you!

Just Plain Bob
justplainbob@awesomeauthors.org

You may also like the books by these authors:

Step Desires

Backscratching Needs

Hot Taboo Erotica

I've always loved getting my back scratched. This is what would lead me into the steamy darkness of a wonderful, sensuous relationship with my stepmother in my adult life. That feeling of nice sharp fingernails dragged gently, softly down my back always soothed me,even when I was a child... even when I was quite an adult.

When I was a child, my mother used to scratch my back long and lovingly. It was one of my earliest memories. Mother died when I was only 7, and I have very few clear memories of her. But the feeling, that slow sensual scratching—softly, almost tickling—for long periods in the evening in front of the TV or the fire on cold nights, always reminds me of her.

I was nearing the end of 2nd grade when Mother had dropped me off at school. I was a bit late so I had to run inside, and missed the carnage when—pulling out onto the busy boulevard—Mother's little Toyota import was utterly crushed under a speeding cement truck. She was killed instantly. But her remains were in such a state that my father's identification of her body was something that traumatized and broke him forever. He would sometimes have flashbacks and nightmares years after. My entire young life was marked by tragedy.

Dad remarried. She was a woman who had been a family friend before her husband had run off, Jeanne Potter; she and I bonded almost instantly. Jeanne and Mom had been friends since high school. In her previous marriage, Jeanne and Dean Potter had a rough go of it. He drank and was a bit of a deadbeat. They had wanted kids, but she couldn't conceive—and he treated her badly because of it.

Jeanne had always adored me. As a close friend of my mother's, she had also been traumatized by her death—and had scooped me up the moment she heard the news. She picked up on my love of having my back scratched immediately. It helped soothe me through the loss of my mother. Perhaps it soothed us both. Dad and she were much thrown together after Mom's passing. They fell in love; maybe they had secretly been—who knows? My new stepmother, Jeanne Anderson, (she couldn't wait to take my father's name), was never a replacement for my real mother, but came an incredibly close second. At their wedding, I asked innocently if I could call her Mom. She had burst into tears and got down on her knees in her pretty white wedding dress and hugged me fiercely. It was never quite the same for her and my brother.

Jeanne, my new "Mom", and I have been thereafter always close—in a way that she wasn't with my brother. She and Dad had always had a very loving, affectionate relationship. I was more like her and Daniel was more like Dad. Not that my brother Daniel got along great with Dad, they were just more similar and had similar interests. They were into cars and sports. I was more into being quiet and reading, playing by myself when I got tired of the neighborhood kids. Jeanne had been like that, or so she told me.

Daniel was older than me by three years, but the age gap seemed much greater. There was no way he would ever allow his bookish younger brother to hang around with him and his friends. I didn't have lots of friends, but they were markedly different—bookish, nerdy, creative. Jeanne and my Dad worried a bit that we weren't closer, but had no idea how to make it better.

One spring, in my 18th year, they decided to take the family on a trip to the mountains of Colorado. Forced to be together, with no one else to hang out with, it was assumed we would bond a bit, being mainly in the great outdoors. Jeanne wasn't really into camping that much. Dad and Daniel were and often went camping, just the two of them. A few times, we had gone tent camping as a family, which was fun, but still not our favorite thing. This trip was to include a two night camp out in the wilderness. Not too wild, as you could drive right to the campsite.

Jeanne and I made camp while Dad and Danny went exploring. They had worked to get us to go, but the day was mostly gone and Jeanne wanted to start dinner. I had noticed the exquisitely cute girl two sites over and was more interested in her than humping it up to the falls. It was chilly out, being spring. The snow had only melted a month before and the river was flowing heavily. I started the fire while Jeanne started dinner. I set up the chairs and made a reasonably cozy campsite.

Afterwards I strolled up the bank of the river, mostly to get a closer look at the cute blonde with her hair pulled up into a sexy knot at the back of her head. She glanced over at me a couple of times as I passed, and her brilliant blue eyes made my heart pound. In a short time I was half a mile up the river. I sat in the slanting evening sunlight, at the edge of the pounding water, as the sun slipped lower and touched the mountains. I thought I had better head back as I had no flashlight if it got dark on me.

It was getting dark by the time I got back, expecting a telling off about being late for dinner. I strolled into the campsite and saw Jeanne/Mom sitting there alone by the dwindling fire, arms around her knees.

"Where did you get off to?" she asked, a slight edge to her voice. I told her that I was just up the river, watching the sunset. "Where the hell are your father and brother?" she asked no one in particular, her voice very edgy now. "They leave us to handle everything here, and simply head off by themselves. Plus, dinner is ready. It's getting cold!"

"We should just eat then," I told her, sitting in the chair next to her. "Let *them* eat cold food." She agreed and we did, sitting quietly munching chili and potato salad, pickles and garlic bread. "They're going to love this garlic bread cold," I muttered. Mom laughed. She asked me to clean our plates as she was going to set up her and Dad's bedding, and disappeared into the huge 12-man tent that we used for car camping.

I cleaned our plates and stuff by the glare of the Coleman lantern, and then went in and started setting up my air mattress and sleeping bag. I left Daniel's, rolled up by the side of the tent. We busied ourselves with these minor chores while we waited. We then went back to the fire and waited some more. Mom was really getting mad about them taking off and being gone so long.

"Did they take flashlights?" she finally asked. I told her that I didn't know. She seemed genuinely worried now, so I got up to check the stock in the box where all there lights were kept. They were all still there. I returned and told her so. "God damn it!" she swore exasperated. "Do you think they went way out and got stuck in the dark?" I agreed that it was possible, but reminded her that Dad was always prepared. He must have taken a small headlamp at least.

We sat by the fire awhile longer, adding logs and staying warm. "We could go look for them," I offered. Mom asked if I even knew which way they went. "Well, they headed up the river. I assume they were headed for the falls. Follow the river and we'll probably find them." She agreed. We sat a while longer. Mom kept looking over her shoulder up the river, as if expecting them to wander into the firelight any moment.

We sat there for another hour, chatting quietly about the trip so far, my relationship with my brother, school, that girl two sites over. She chided me over my shyness around girls and we both laughed a bit, but she was increasingly uncomfortable about Dad and Daniel being gone so long. I knew she was going to give them such a telling off when they got back.

"Should we go check with the rangers?" she wondered. I told her that the station was closed when I passed, but that they were probably cruising around. I would flag them down when they went by. We sat in silence now, staring into the flames. It was really getting late. Clearly, something was wrong. They must really be lost.

"I hope that none of them got hurt," she said quietly, sounding very distressed. Moments later the headlights from the ranger truck flashed on us as it approached. We both jumped out of our chairs. We flagged him down and explained the situation. He introduced himself as Ranger Mike and asked what time they had set out. We told him the time and he calculated that they would have just reached the falls at sunset, but that they would have passed the upper ranger station to get there. Perhaps it got too dark and they holed up there, he wondered. He got on the radio and called the ranger upriver, had he seen the two guys pass by? The ranger responded that he had and warned them that it was getting dark. His voice sounded irked that the yahoos had given him a 'Yeah, yeah, yeah.' reply and continued on.

Both rangers sounded a bit put out that now they had two people lost in the dark. They agreed that they would set out in the dark and go find them. Our ranger, Mike, told us to hang tight and wait for them to bring the guys in. We gave him their names and descriptions, and he headed off to arrange a search party, telling us to sit tight and not go anywhere. They didn't need more people going missing in the dark.

Mom and I returned to the fire to wait. Mom was really mad by now, but nervous at the same time. I could tell she was hoping that they were just lost, a stupid thing, and not hurt. She would give them such grief later.

By now it was midnight and we were both nodding off by the fire. "Screw this!" she said angrily. "I'm freezing. Let's go to bed. They can wake us up when they get back." She stood and marched to the tent, unzipping it roughly. I banked the fire a bit and followed. I went in and turned to zip it closed. Mom stood there staring at the two sleeping bags that she had zipped together for her and Dad. "Well, your father isn't here to keep me warm, so why don't you climb in with me?" It wasn't really a question.

I watched as she quickly tossed off her jacket and shucked off her jeans. She was wearing silk long johns, top and bottom, and pulled a Flashdance move, unhooking and removing her bra from underneath her shirt…

If you enjoyed this sample then look for **Step Desires**.

HOT EROTICA

HIRED FOR
Their Pleasure

A LATE BLOOMER'S 1ST TIME

JACK RYDER

"Mom was right, you have a gorgeous body," her voice startled me awake. I guess I must have stirred a bit when my body felt the pressure of someone sitting down on the bed next to me. I was still a bit groggy as I open my eyes to see Katie sitting there staring down at me. It took a few moments for to remember that I was completely naked. I instinctively reached to pull the blankets up but found that they had been kicked off onto the floor at some point in my sleep.

"Should I lock the door from now on, or is it acceptable for me to be naked every time you barge into my house unannounced?" My voice was hoarse and strained. I could see a look of lust on her face as she gawked at my flaccid prick. "You can be naked any time I come over," she told me with her eyes never leaving my dick. "Besides, Mom told you I would be over for breakfast." I glanced at the clock and it was ten after 9am.

"Do you think I'm pretty, Jake?" She whispered. "Oh hell yes, Katie...you are so very sexy," I told her as I felt a slight wiggle. Kathleen was wearing that tiny white bikini again. The way she was seated with one leg dangling off the bed and the other leg bent beside her, left her legs spread wide apart and I could see her pussy lips pressed tight against the crotch of her bottoms.

"But, I'm so skinny and I have no tits," she complained softly. "Even Stevie has bigger tits than I have," she lamented. "Are you kidding me?" I chuckled. "With that sexy slender body, those perky cone shaped tits are perfect." I gasped. "There are many men that prefer perky tits rather than the big globe type," I informed her. "You are incredibly sexy just the way you are, sweetie."

"Do you think you could like these as much as my mother's?" Katie reached up and untied her top so it fell forward to expose her breasts to me. "Ooooh Katie, look at you," I gasped as she reached back to undo the other string and her top fell off. Her small 32A cone shaped tits were less than a foot from my face. Her pink puffy nipples were exactly the same as her mother's but seemed more pronounced since her tits are more cone shaped. She also had those pure white triangles from her bikini tan line that has always aroused me deeply. "Damn, those are sexy," I gasped.

My dick had become fully rigid within seconds as I gazed at her exposed tits. "I see you're telling the truth," she giggled as she watched my dick bouncing against my belly. "You can touch them if you like," she whispered as she scooted a little closer and pulled her other leg up onto the bed. My hands were trembling noticeably as I reached forward to fondle both of her nubile little tits.

"That feels wonderful, Jake," she purred softly as she arched her back to press her breast firmly into my hands. I let go of her left breast and used placed my right hand around her waist so I could pull her forward. "Yes Jake, Yessssss," she moaned as I wrapped my lips around her left puffy pink nipple and began to gently suck on it.

I felt her moving slightly and then felt her right hand wrapping around my rigid prick. "It's so big," she cooed when she saw that she could barely get her hand all the way around my girth. "Oooh, God Yes," I moaned as she started to gently stroke up and down my shaft. "So good, Jake, it feels s-o-o-o-o good," she gasped when I moved my mouth to suck on her other nipple.

My legs were quivering on the bed as she slowly jerked me off while I feasted on both of her perky tits. "I was so hard for you yesterday," I confessed as she got me closer and closer to orgasm. "You made my meat so wet when you were modeling those clothes," she answered me with a moan.

If you enjoyed this sample then look for **Hired For Their Pleasure**.

HOT EROTICA, BDSM

The
Mistress
AND THE PET

EMILY SPARROW

Thirteen years ago I joined a private dungeon group in Seattle, Washington and had attended several parties held there and had never met anyone like Mistress. It was a Friday night and the theme that night was take down play. I am not sure if you know what this type of play involves. In a nutshell, anything goes in this play. It is usually reserved for the most extreme playing or to teach someone a lesson that was not learned before.

I had a chance before to play with others as I come to the dungeon alone and the scenes always drew an audience. You see, I love pain...cannot get enough of it. It does not matter to me what is done as long as nothing is broken and I do not require a trip to the emergency room after playing. So the scenes I was involved with became quite messy with my blood from being whipped or having needles stuck into my most private spots and various other tortures I endured.

Tonight as before, I sought out the Events Director and told her I would like to play if someone was looking. I wandered about the room watching subs and slaves being put through their paces...hearing their screams...the sounds of whips and canes striking their flesh. I do not see many males here tonight and I like that as it meant I might have a better chance at the rough playing I needed.

My wandering brought me to the far corner of the dungeon where a very pretty woman about 33 was strapped face down upon a sawhorse type of apparatus with her wrists and ankles secured tightly along the legs of the horse. There were 2 men at each end of her, one ramming her ass and the other pumping her mouth with a steady rhythm going. There was a woman wearing a black leather corset and black garter with thigh high nylons standing next to them. This woman wore no panties and had a neatly shaved vagina that peeked out from under the garter affair she wore. As the men fucked the helpless woman on the horse, the other woman was whipping her hard across her back and shoulders. Her back was crisscrossed with dozens of stripes looking very red and some almost purple. Blood oozed from many of the whip marks.

I was so enthralled by this scene I was not aware the Event Director was calling my name. I kind of jumped a little when she touched me on my shoulder and I turned to see her standing there with another woman I had never seen before. She introduced her as Miss Sarah and left us alone. This woman was beautiful with long flowing dark brown hair and deep blue eyes. She had an ample bosom, tight waist, long, shapely legs. The most striking thing about her was the long elegant evening dress she was wearing. More suited to being at a fancy ball then a dungeon. Miss Sarah had been watching the scene I was and had a chance to watch my reactions also. As she stood beside me she asked my name and I replied, "Miss Sarah I am David". We talked for 20 minutes while watching the whipping continue and I was asked many questions about my likes and dislikes and what I hoped to find here tonight.

I told Miss Sarah what my limits were. While I did this I looked her in the eyes and I could almost see a fire glowing from inside her. I shrugged it off as my over active imagination playing tricks on me. Miss Sarah reached her hand out and stroked my broad chest and it was almost like being touched with an electric current. It took my breath away and I felt my knees quiver just a little. I had never felt this way from being touched before now.

Miss Sarah eyed me and watched my expressions as she asked if I really wanted to play with her tonight. I almost screamed out my answer but managed to hold back and told her, "Miss Sarah I would like to play with you."

She placed her hand in mine and walked away from this scene to the various restraint sections of the dungeon until we stopped at a huge wooden X shaped thing. The beams were 10 feet long and made of solid oak 8 inches square. Each beam had 12 eyehooks bolted into it and was impossible to pull loose from the wood. The top and bottoms of the beams were secured to the roof beams and wooden floor and would not tip over no matter how hard someone would struggle.

If you enjoyed this sample then look for **The Mistress And The Pet**.

EROTIC ROMANCE

Teaching
SARA LOVE

Rocky Austin Quinn

"Jay! Phone!" I called out to my roommate Jay who was packing for a trip to Florida.

"Who is it?" He yelled back.

"Sara!"

Jay came walking into the room with a worried look on his face.

"No, it can't be this week," he said as he grabbed the phone. "Hello, Sara? Please tell me you - you are at the airport now. Damn, I could have sworn you were coming next week. I have a wedding to go to, I'll be gone all weekend. I know you can't fly back - I'm sure -," he looked at me. "I'm sure Chris won't mind hanging out with you for the week," he quietly said as he walked out of the room.

I'm sure that Sara was not thrilled about spending the weekend with me. It's not like we have issues with each other, we just have not really met before. I have probably said three words to her, all over the phone. Jay came back into the room and put the phone on the table.

"Listen man, I didn't know that Sara was coming this week. I need you to keep her entertained for the next few days. I'm the only person she knows in this state and I don't want her staying alone in a hotel room or something," Jay said as he ran back to the bedroom and grabbed his suitcase. "You can pick her up after you drop me off."

"No problem, I'm sure we could find something to do," I said while standing up and grabbing my car keys. "Let's go."

Jay grabbed me by the arm and stopped me.

"I owe you man. Just be nice to my cousin, she can be a little shy. My aunt and uncle are very strict parents and she isn't great at making friends. She won't really open up unless she trusts you," he told me in a serious tone.

"Don't worry; I'll make her feel at home," I said with a smile.

We left the apartment and headed downstairs to my old Ford Taurus. Jay loaded his suitcase in the back and climbed aboard. We headed off for what should have been a half-hour drive to Los Angeles International Airport. It was noon on a Friday so the traffic heading into the city was a mess, not that it isn't a pain all day every day.

After a delay, we arrived at the airport just shy of 1:00 in the afternoon. His flight was not until 3:00 so he still had plenty of time to get through security. I followed him around the airport until he found Sara. I had never seen her before so I had no idea what to expect. She was a pretty short girl, probably no taller than five-foot three. She was definitely cute, not drop-dead gorgeous but very cute and innocent-looking with long black hair that had two blond streaks running down the front. I could not tell how her body looked since she was wearing baggy black jeans and a loose-fitting black hoodie.

Jay and Sara hugged and talked for a few minutes before walking towards me.

"Chris, this is Sara. Sara, this is Chris," Jay said.

"Hi," she softly said, visibly shy.

I could see that her mouth was fitted with braces.

"Hi Sara," I responded.

"Well guys, I got to head off," said my roommate. "See you guys in a week."

Jay headed towards security and left me alone with his cousin.

"Come on Chris, let's get out of here," Sara said while forcing a smile before following me outside.

For the entire hour long ride home, Sara looked out the window and said nothing. Since Jay had told me that she was extremely shy, I did not try to force anything. I knew that when she wanted to talk, she would talk.

Once we made it out of the city, we finally started making good time. In no time, we were at the apartment. I got out of the car and started towards the door but Sara remained in her seat. I walked over and knocked on the window, causing her to jump. She looked up at me from inside.

"Sorry," she said.

I opened the door for her.

"No need to apologize," I told her as I grabbed her bags from the backseat and led her inside.

If you enjoyed this sample then look for <u>Teaching Sara Love</u>.

CHOSEN TO BE

Christy's

EXTRA LOVER

HOT SEXY EROTICA

JOAN VEGAS

As I pondered what Ben was asking me about setting up a gang bang for Christy, I knew Andy and Mark would eagerly join in. But how would I discretely recruit other guys? Ben was asking me to line up at least 6 guys, in addition to me and him. I told Ben I would try. He wanted me to set it up about 5 or 6 weeks later, when he knew he would be home. And, he told me to not mention anything to Christy about our plans. He wanted to surprise her.

A few days later, I told Mark and Andy about my mission for Christy. When I told them they would be invited, they whooped and hollered. They both said they could hardly wait. I asked if they had any suggestions on how I could line up four more guys. They both suggested other guys at our school. I wasn't so sure I wanted other guys from our school knowing about the sweet deal I had with Christy and Ben.

Then Mark suggested that we put a discrete ad in one of the local alternative newspapers that was read by younger people throughout the Chicago area. After mulling over the idea, we pooled our money to place this ad for a couple of weeks: "Pretty gal wants more than one guy…soon. Write to P. O. Box ___ for details."

To our happy surprise, one of the newspapers took our ad. A week after the paper came out, the three of us got together to open the replies we had received. Wow…9 of them. Some of them included face and/or dick pictures. I was amazed. We set aside replies from older guys and married guys. We designated four of them as good prospects.

The next week, we received eleven more replies. Most of them had understood that "The pretty gal" was looking for a gang bang. They were all eager to participate. That time, we ruled out seven of them. That left us with a total of eight prospects (not counting Mark, Andy and me). I decided to contact Ben and get his opinion before we met with any of the respondents.

Again Ben and I met for a beer…alone. I told him I had two friends who were enthusiastic about the idea of helping to fulfill Christy's wish. Then I gave him the eight envelopes we had selected. He agreed that ten guys (plus he and I) might be a bit overwhelming for Christy. He set aside three of the envelopes and said, "How about if you and your friends 'interview' these other five guys." I agreed, and we finished our beers.

That evening, Ben and I had lots of fun with Christy as we winked at each other when she was turned away, knowing what we were planning for her. We made sure she got her share of orgasms that night before we each drained our nuts inside her velvety love channel.

The next day Andy, Mark and I met. I told them about Ben's decisions. We decided on a bar where we could discretely meet with the selected guys…one at a time over the next several days. They each took two guys to call, and I took one. One of Mark's contacts proved to be a flake, so we dropped him.

Over the next week, we met individually with the four remaining guys. They all seemed clean, discrete, and personable. Most importantly, they were all very eager to share in fulfilling "Mindy's" desire to be screwed by several guys. (Yes, we changed Christy's name so no one could ever come back on her.) We got their contact phone numbers, told them the tentative time, and told them we would be calling with a hotel location where we would be meeting.

Ben arranged for a hotel suite and told Christy to be ready for an extra special evening with me and him giving her lots of passionate loving. She bought it.

Shortly after Ben and Christy arrived in the hotel room, I came in (I had my own key card). He and I necked with her while stripping off her clothes. We got her onto the middle of the large bed and Ben began to eat her. I told them I had to go get some ice for our drinks, and left Christy to enjoy Ben's oral ministrations.

I ran downstairs and met Mark and Andy. I brought them to the suite and had them quietly remove their clothes as I made noise mixing drinks for Christy and Ben. In the background, Andy and Mark were both stroking themselves to hardness. I walked into the bedroom with a drink in each hand saying, "You guys ready for some liquid refreshment?" They both sat up and reached for a drink.

Then I looked at Christy and asked, "Are you ready for some extra pleasure?" That was my cue to Mark and Andy. They walked in behind me, totally naked, with boners sticking out in front of them. I said, "Christy...this is Mark and this Andy...my friends...here to give you some extra pleasure." Christy grinned at my nude friends. Ben had already stood up. He said, "Christy baby, I hope you enjoy this special evening," and he sat in a nearby chair.

Andy dove between Christy's outstretched legs and began to lick on her pussy. Although I was still dressed, I got on the bed, cuddled Christy into my arms, and gave her a big kiss. Meanwhile, Mark laid on the bed on the other side of Christy and began caressing her body. He took one of her hands and wrapped it around his stiff dick.

Christy whispered into my ear, "What's going on?" I told her, "Tonight you are going to get your vagina eaten and screwed to your heart's content. Enjoy yourself." She grinned at me before rolling to face Mark. "You are Mark, huh?" she said, while squeezing his dick. "My," she said, "your dick is very hard. I'll bet you know how to use it." She threw her arm over his shoulder and gave him a hot kiss.

If you enjoyed this sample then look for <u>Chosen To Be Christy's Extra Lover</u>.

WANT FREE COPIES OF MY BOOKS?

Just visit my blog and download free copies of my books:

awesomeauthors.org/justplainbob

www.ingramcontent.com/pod-product-compliance
Lightning Source LLC
Chambersburg PA
CBHW071413170626
46811CB00003B/1378